HEAVY MACHINES

Debbie Croft

Contents

What Are Heavy Machines? 2
Keeping Safe near Heavy Machines 12
How a House Site Is Prepared 14
Glossary 23
Index 24

What Are Heavy Machines?

Bulldozers, graders, cranes and excavators are large, heavy machines. These machines are used for making roads, clearing areas of bushland and preparing building sites. At **quarries**, some of these machines move large amounts of rock and soil.

a crane at a building site

Graders and cranes are carried on trailers when they need to move long distances.

Some graders and cranes can be driven short distances on roads, but they can only travel very slowly. Bulldozers and excavators are moved from place to place on a long trailer pulled by a large truck.

Bulldozers

Bulldozers are special types of tractors. They are very powerful, and usually have metal tracks instead of rubber tyres. Metal tracks allow these machines to be driven across rough or uneven ground more easily.

A bulldozer has a huge metal **blade** at the front of the machine. This blade can be used to move large amounts of soil, sand or rubbish to clear an area of land.

Think and Talk About …

Metal tracks help to stop bulldozers from sinking into soft or muddy ground.

a bulldozer

The ripper on the back of a bulldozer helps to break up rocks on the ground.

There is a long claw at the back of the bulldozer, called a "ripper". The ripper is used to loosen rocks and large pieces of concrete near the surface of the ground. This waste material can be pushed out of the way with the blade of the bulldozer. Then, the waste is loaded onto trucks and taken to recycling centres.

Bulldozers are very useful at quarries or mines. After sand, rock or **minerals** have been removed from the ground, a bulldozer **levels** the area again so new trees can be planted. Bulldozers are also used in road building and for clearing land on building sites.

Graders

Graders are heavy machines that are used to make a flat surface on a road or block of land. Most graders have three **axles**. The engine and driver's cab are at the back of the machine, above the two rear axles. A third axle is at the front of the grader. There is a long, narrow blade between the front and back axles.

Graders are often used to make or repair gravel roads. First, the area has to be cleared. The driver lowers the blade until it touches the ground. As the grader moves forward, the blade pushes grass, small rocks and loose soil off the roadway.

A grader is used to make uneven ground smooth.

Then, the road is graded again. Dirt gets pushed along by the blade. It falls into hollows in the road, making the surface smooth and even.

Next, trucks are used to bring loads of fine gravel to the site. This gravel is tipped in piles along the road so it can be spread by the grader in an even layer. Then, a roller is driven along the road several times to make the surface hard. Now the road is safer for traffic to use.

Think and Talk About …

The blade on a grader can be set higher on one side than the other, so the graded area is not completely level.

Cranes

Cranes are large machines that are used to move heavy objects. These objects can weigh much more than the crane itself. Cables or chains on the crane are attached to the load to lift it into position.

Cranes that can be driven from one location to another are called "mobile" cranes. Sometimes, a mobile crane might only be used to shift one heavy load at a site. Then, the crane is taken to another location.

Other cranes are called "fixed" cranes, because they are used in the same place for a long time. On some sites, these cranes are put on a **platform** beside a tall building. Large blocks of concrete or metal beams can be lifted up the sides of these buildings using fixed cranes.

Think and Talk About ...

Cranes on building sites are moved further up the side of the building as each storey is completed.

Sometimes, cranes are needed to bring heavy objects from the top of a building to the ground. Cranes are very useful when buildings have to be pulled down.

Some goods are transported by road, rail or sea in large metal containers that are very heavy. Cranes are needed at **wharves** and railway yards to load and unload these goods.

Cranes are used to move heavy objects from place to place.

Excavators

Excavators are heavy machines, too. Different sized excavators are used for different types of jobs. Small excavators are suitable for digging drains in house yards where there is not a lot of space. Bigger excavators dig out soil and sand in quarries.
The biggest excavators have enormous buckets that can move massive amounts of rock or soil in a short time.

An excavator has large metal tracks. These help to keep the machine **stable** when it is driven on rough or muddy ground.

The top part of an excavator is called the "house". The driver can **swivel** the house to the left or the right without moving the tracks. The house also includes the driver's cab, the "boom", the "stick" and the bucket. The boom and stick are like an arm that can reach a long way from the machine.

The bucket on an excavator can move large amounts of rock or soil.

Think and Talk About …

The driver can swivel the excavator in a full circle in either direction.

The driver sits in the cab and uses levers and **joysticks** to work the machine. The levers drive the machine backwards and forwards along the ground. One joystick moves the boom and stick. They can go in and out, or up and down. This joystick also lifts and lowers the bucket.

The second joystick is used to swivel the house. A bucketload of material can be dug out of the ground on one side of the machine. Then, the driver swivels the house so the bucket can be emptied into a truck on the other side of the machine. Often, many trucks can be loaded without needing to move the whole excavator.

Keeping Safe near Heavy Machines

Bulldozers, graders, cranes and excavators are large machines that are used to do heavy work. People using these machines need to have special training so they can operate them safely. Workers must always wear proper safety clothing and equipment when they work with heavy machines.

How a House Site Is Prepared

The area of land where a house is to be built is called a house site. This area of land must be properly prepared before workers start to build the house.

If the house site is on a farm or a similar property, a bulldozer and an excavator are used to clear the land.

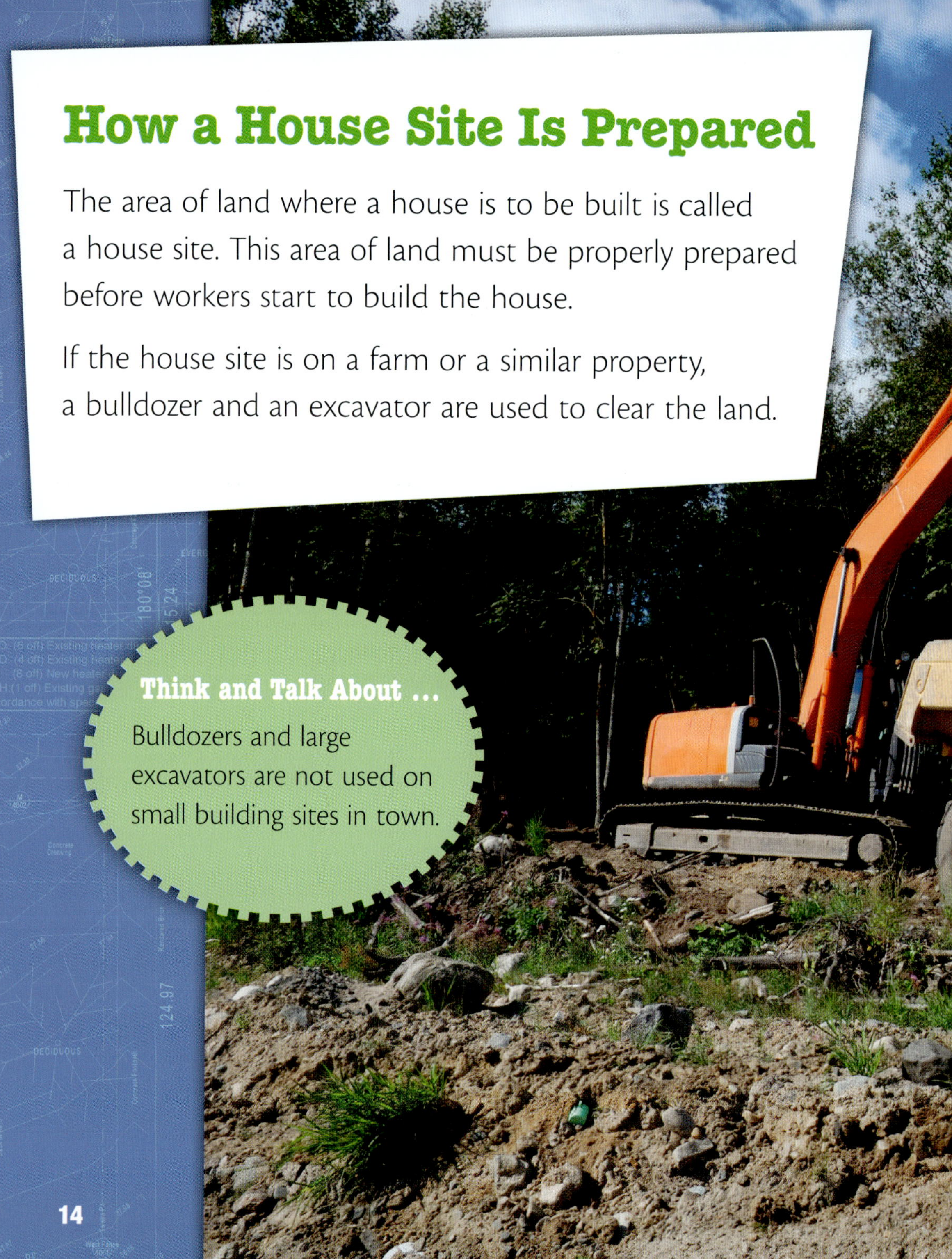

Think and Talk About ...

Bulldozers and large excavators are not used on small building sites in town.

First, all the trees that are growing on the site have to be removed. The bulldozer is a very powerful machine, so the blade is used to push the trees and roots out of the ground. If the roots break off, they are dug out using the excavator.

Next, the driver uses the bucket of the excavator to drag soil into the holes where the trees have been taken out. Then, grass, bushes and a small amount of soil are scraped away by the bulldozer to make the area flat.

Think and Talk About ...

The owners of the new house can plant some trees in the garden when the building is finished.

When the area has been cleared, the place where the house will be built is marked with wooden pegs. These pegs are hammered into the ground to show exactly where the corners of the building will be. Sometimes, the house site is on sloping ground. The pegs also have marks so the workers can be sure that the floor of the house will be level.

Then, the excavator is used to dig out some of the soil within the pegged area. This soil is not suitable to use on the building site. It is usually taken away from where the house will be built.

HM30

Next, special soil, called "fill" soil, is delivered to the building site in large trucks. These trucks dump the soil into the area that has been dug out by the excavator. This fill soil is used because it can be **compacted**. It provides a very solid base so the **foundations** of the house are strong.

Then, the fill material is spread across the site using the excavator. The driver checks that the fill soil comes up to the mark on each of the pegs. Finally, a heavy roller is driven across the fill soil many times.

When the soil is properly compacted, the site is finished and building can begin.

Glossary

axles (*noun*)	the bars that connect and turn the wheels of a vehicle
blade (*noun*)	a long, flat piece of metal
compacted (*verb*)	made flat and packed tightly
foundations (*noun*)	the bottom part or base of a building
joysticks (*noun*)	sticks that are used to control moving parts of a machine
levels (*verb*)	makes flat and even
minerals (*noun*)	substances that are naturally formed in the ground
platform (*noun*)	a flat surface that is raised above the ground
quarries (*noun*)	big pits in the ground for digging up stone for building
stable (*adjective*)	steady and balanced
swivel (*verb*)	to turn or spin
wharves (*noun*)	places where ships can load and unload

Index

axle 6, 23
blade 4–7, 16, 23
bucket 10–11, 16
building site 2, 5, 8, 15, 19–20
bulldozer 2–5, 13–17, 21
cab 6, 10–11
crane 2–3, 8–9, 13
excavator 2–3, 10–16, 18–19, 21–22
fill soil 21–22
grader 2–3, 6–7, 13
joystick 11, 23
lever 11
quarry 2, 5, 10, 23
ripper 5
rock 2, 5–6, 10
roller 7, 22
soil 2, 4–6, 10–11, 16, 19–22
tracks 4, 10
trailer 3
truck 3, 5, 7, 11, 20–21